This Walker book belongs to:

_____

_____

_____

For Milo Robertson, with love.

And for all the lovely, fluffy people out there
who've ever felt that they were unravelling.

First published 2009 by Walker Books Ltd
87 Vauxhall Walk, London SE11 5HJ

This edition published 2010

2 4 6 8 10 9 7 5 3 1

© 2009 Jan Fearnley

The right of Jan Fearnley to be identified as author/illustrator of this work has been asserted by
her in accordance with the Copyright, Designs and Patents Act 1988

This book has been typeset in Lucida Grande

Printed in China

All rights reserved. No part of this book may be reproduced, transmitted or stored in an informa-
tion retrieval system in any form or by any means, graphic, electronic or mechanical, including
photocopying, taping and recording, without prior written permission from the publisher.

British Library Cataloguing in Publication Data:
a catalogue record for this book is available from the British Library

ISBN 978-1-4063-2555-3

www.walker.co.uk

WALKER BOOKS
AND SUBSIDIARIES
LONDON · BOSTON · SYDNEY · AUCKLAND

Milo Armadillo

Jan Fearnley

When it was nearly Tallulah's birthday, her parents asked her what she would like for a present.

"I want a pink fluffy rabbit," said Tallulah.

You'd think it would be easy
to find a pink fluffy rabbit.

But it wasn't.

In the toyshop, there was a pink elephant, a pink doll, a pink hippopotamus and a pink pelican.

"I want a pink fluffy rabbit!"
said Tallulah.

In the pet shop, there were grey rabbits,

brown rabbits,

white rabbits

and spotty rabbits.

"All I want is a pink fluffy rabbit,"

said Tallulah.

Tallulah searched everywhere but she had no luck.

"Just one pink fluffy rabbit,"
sighed Tallulah.

"Is it too much to ask?"

Then Gran had a brilliant idea.
"I'll make one,"
she said.

Gran took some
needles and fuzzy pink
yarn and started knitting...

clickety - click

clickety - click

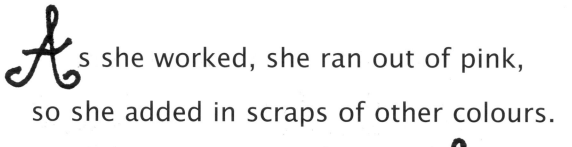

As she worked, she ran out of pink,
so she added in scraps of other colours.

clickety - click

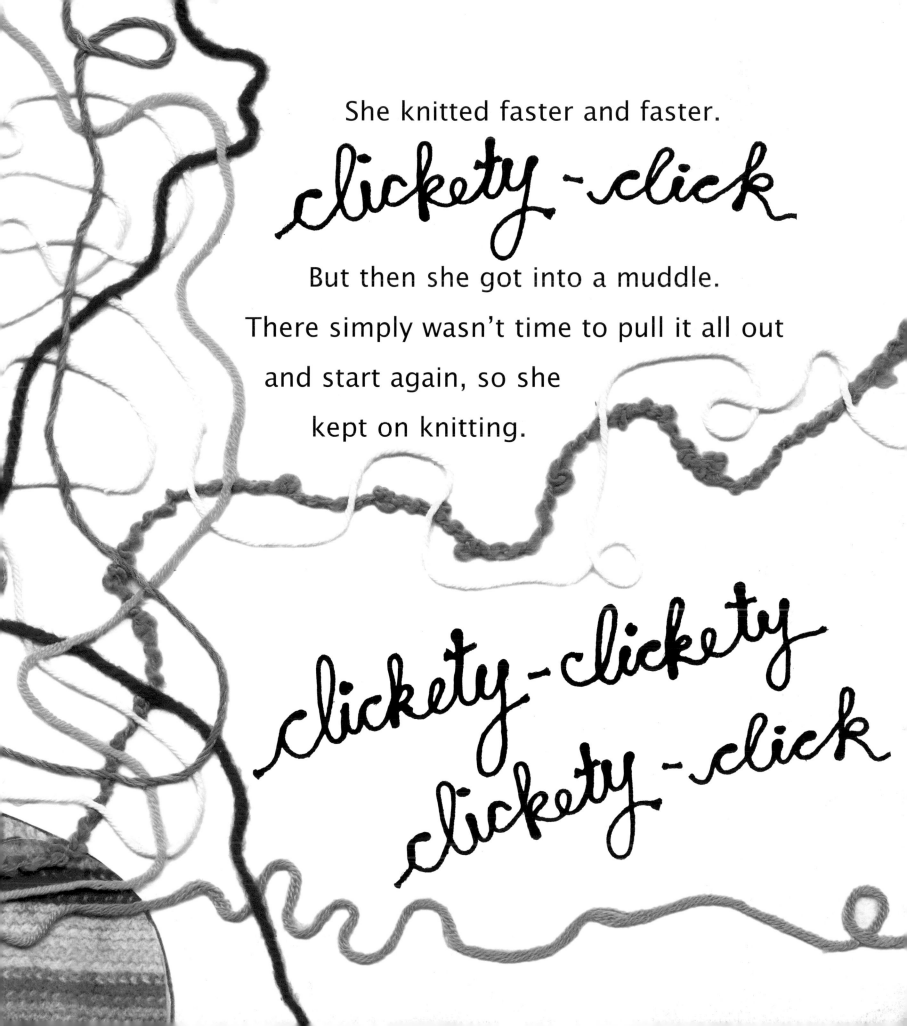

She knitted faster and faster.

clickety - click

But then she got into a muddle.

There simply wasn't time to pull it all out

and start again, so she

kept on knitting.

clickety - clickety

clickety - click

W hen she had finished, instead of a pink fluffy rabbit, Gran ended up with something very different.

"Perfect!" chuckled Gran.

She liked what she'd done.

"You're cute and pink and fluffy," she said.

"I shall call you M*lo."

Tallulah gasped with excitement
when she saw a pink fluffy something
peeping out of the box.

"**Hooray!** It's a pink ... fluffy ...

"This is Milo Armadillo," said Gran.

Tallulah felt disappointed.

She'd really wanted a rabbit,

but she didn't want to hurt Gran's feelings.

"He's lovely!" she said.

He wasn't a pink fluffy rabbit,

but Gran had clearly gone

to a lot of trouble.

Milo Armadillo would have to do.

At first, Tallulah and Milo
got to know each other.

Milo Armadillo was sporty.

"That's good jumping," said Tallulah,

"but rabbits jump higher."

Milo Armadillo played funky tunes.

"Very good," said Tallulah airily,
"but rabbits only play
classical music."

They sailed away on amazing adventures.
"This is fun," said Tallulah, "but rabbits
are jolly good sailors too, you know."

As the days
went by

they played
lots of games
together

and shared stories and fun.

Even so, Tallulah couldn't stop wondering about pink fluffy rabbits.

"He's funny-looking," said Tallulah's friends (who ALL had pink fluffy rabbits).

"He's different," they said.

"He's an Armadillo," said Tallulah.

"He's cute," said her friends.

"But he's no pink fluffy rabbit,"
 sighed Tallulah.

Milo Armadillo heard every word.

He resolved to make Tallulah happy.

He went to the beauty parlour.

He asked for "the works".

But he still didn't look anything like a pink fluffy rabbit.

He went to the fancy dress shop and bought a disguise.

But instead of looking like a pink fluffy rabbit, he just looked silly.

*M*ilo Armadillo felt sad.

He could do so many clever things,

but he couldn't be a pink fluffy rabbit.

It just wasn't possible.

Or was it?

He decided to run away to Gran
and ask her to unravel him.

Then she could knit the wool
into a proper pink fluffy
rabbit for Tallulah.

It was the only thing
he could do.

Sadly, he crept away.

When Tallulah got home from school that day,
she was bursting with things to tell and show.
But when she called, there was no answer.
Milo Armadillo had gone.

There was nobody to share stories
or play with. There was only
a sad, empty feeling.

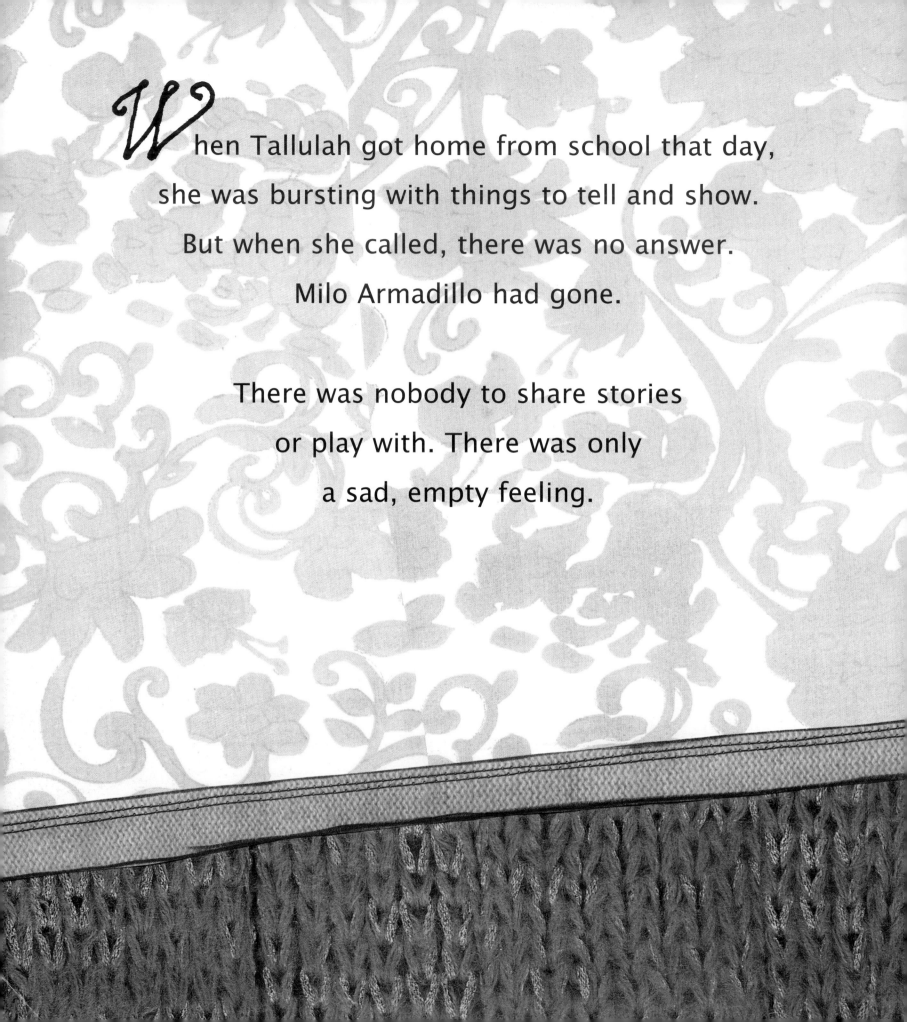

Tallulah realized she'd lost something *very special*.

"Never mind, dear,"
said Tallulah's mother.
"Now you can have a
pink fluffy rabbit."

"I don't WANT a pink fluffy rabbit," cried Tallulah. "I want *Milo Armadillo*".

Then she saw a pink thread...

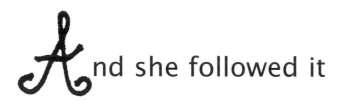And she followed it

all the way ...

until she found him.

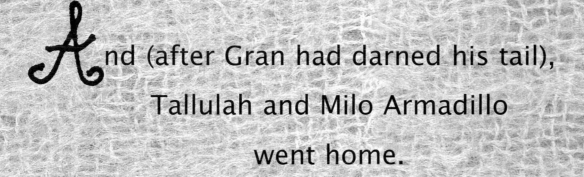

And (after Gran had darned his tail),
Tallulah and Milo Armadillo
went home.

Other books by Jan Fearnley

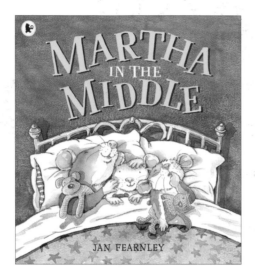

978-1-4063-1953-8

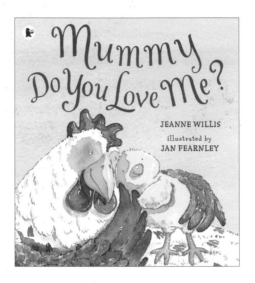

978-1-4063-1765-7

978-1-4063-0601-9

978-0-7445-9650-2

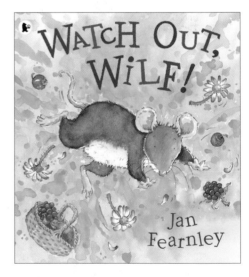

978-1-84428-509-9

Available from all good bookstores

www.walker.co.uk